This igloo book belongs to:

....

Published in 2016
by Igloo Books Ltd
Cottage Farm,
Sywell,
NN6 0BJ
www.igloobooks.com

GUA006 0316
2 4 6 8 10 9 7 5 3
ISBN: 978-1-78557-091-9

Printed and manufactured in China

My Treasury of
Princess Stories

igloobooks

Contents

The Fairy Queen

Once upon a time, a princess had three older sisters who loved to go to balls and parties. The princess wanted to go too, but she was too young. When her sisters were getting ready to go out, the youngest princess would go off by herself and walk around the fields and hills near the castle.

One day, the princess took a different path than usual and found herself in a wooded glade. The sun was setting and it would soon be dark. The princess knew she had to return home soon. Just as she was about to go back, she saw a glimmer nearby. It was coming from inside a ring of grass.

The princess walked towards the ring and saw pretty girls, who were dressed in white with red caps. They were dancing hand in hand, round the ring. The princess knew this must be a fairy ring because her grandmother had often told her about them. Suddenly, the girls called to the princess, "Come and join the dance!"

As soon as the princess stepped into the ring, she saw a fine lady on a white horse appear, as if from nowhere. The lady wore a dress that was covered in pale, gleaming jewels. Her eyes seemed to glow, just like her jewels. "I am the Fairy Queen," she said. "Won't you come with us, Princess? The party is about to start."

The princess got on the back of the white horse and they rode off to a small hill. As if by magic, the hillside opened and the horse and riders went inside.

The Fairy Queen took the princess into a strange and beautiful forest, where silver trees had fruit, like glass, hanging from their branches. The fruit gave off a pale light and the princess could see three fairy girls playing a harp, a flute, and a violin. All around, fairy folk danced gracefully to the strange, enchanting music.

Fairy waiters moved around the guests, holding plates piled high with delicious-looking cakes and candy. The princess reached out to take a cake, but stopped suddenly. She remembered something her grandmother had once told her—anyone who tasted fairy food, or drink, would be trapped in Fairyland for a hundred years.

The princess danced until late in the night and then she said goodbye to the Fairy Queen. "Please, have a sip of some of our special apple juice before you go," said the Fairy Queen, handing the princess a golden goblet.

The princess refused to take the goblet. "No, thank you, Your Majesty," she said, politely. "I have had a wonderful time. You must come and visit my palace soon."

"Thank you for your invitation," said the Fairy Queen. "We will be at your castle tomorrow night, when the clock chimes eight."

There was a sudden whirl of light and sound. The fairy kingdom disappeared and the princess found herself outside her castle, just as the sun was setting. It was as if no time had passed at all. The princess tried to tell her sisters about the Fairy Queen, but they didn't believe her. "You must have been dreaming," they said.

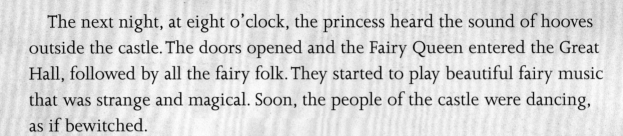

The next night, at eight o'clock, the princess heard the sound of hooves outside the castle. The doors opened and the Fairy Queen entered the Great Hall, followed by all the fairy folk. They started to play beautiful fairy music that was strange and magical. Soon, the people of the castle were dancing, as if bewitched.

The Fairy Queen watched with a smile, while everyone whirled gracefully around. "What pretty people," the princess heard her say. "I will take them all home with me. It will be most amusing to have them in my fairy palace."

"This is my fault," thought the princess. "If I don't do something, everyone will be spirited away to Fairyland." Then the princess had an idea. She raced down to the palace kitchens. There, she found a small piece of brittle candy and made a big hole in it, so that it resembled a ring.

The princess took the candy to the Fairy Queen. "A present for you, Your Majesty," she said, slipping the ring onto the Fairy Queen's finger. But, as soon as it had touched her skin, the ring suddenly crumbled into small candy pieces.

The Fairy Queen licked her finger. "Why, that wasn't a real ring. It was made of sugar. What a strange girl you are. But enough games," said the Fairy Queen, "you are all coming with me to Fairyland."

The Fairy Queen raised her arms to spirit everyone away, but nothing happened. "Where are my powers?" she cried.
"My grandmother told me that fairy magic works both ways," said the princess. "Now that you have tasted mortal food, I'm afraid your powers are lost until you return to Fairyland."

The Fairy Queen looked furious, then amused. She nodded. "Fair is fair, Princess. We will go, but remember, the door in the hill is always open to you." Then in a flash, the fairies were all gone.

When the princess was old enough to go to the palace balls, everyone noticed that she was the finest dancer of them all. Some said it was because her sisters had taught her, but the princess knew it was because she had once danced all night with the Fairy Queen.

The Princess and the Ballerina

Once upon a time, a princess named Rosalind lived in a huge palace with her mother, the queen, and her father, the king. Princess Rosalind loved to dance. All day long, she would twirl and whirl around the palace, standing on tiptoe to show her parents that she was just like a real ballerina. However, no matter how well Rosalind danced, the king and queen never noticed her. They were always busy doing other things around the palace. However, Rosalind was determined that she would dance like a real ballerina.

One day, a troupe of ballet dancers came to the palace to perform for the king. Rosalind was allowed to go and watch them in the Great Hall. The stage was set and the lights went down. Rosalind felt a thrill of excitement as the ballerinas whirled onto the stage and the performance began.

The dancers moved around the stage with beauty and grace. They leaped and spun, as if they were lighter than air. Their dresses shimmered like diamonds in the light. Rosalind was enchanted. At the end of the performance, the dancers bowed and the audience applauded. Some people even stood up and called "Bravo".

One ballerina, who danced like an angel, got the most applause. She wore
a jeweled mask over her face and had flowers in her hair.
"She must be the luckiest girl in the world," thought Rosalind, enviously.
"Everyone loves her. I must meet her."

Nobody noticed Rosalind, as she sneaked behind the stage, where the
dancers were busy changing out of their costumes. Rosalind found the
ballerina taking off her mask. Her name was Ella and she was pale and thin.
Like the princess, she had long, golden hair.
"Nobody notices me," said Rosalind. "I wish I could dance on stage,
like you. Then everyone would finally see me."

"I wish I were a princess like you," said Ella. "Then I would be able to lounge on golden cushions and eat delicious food all day."

The two girls looked at each other and smiled. They both had the same idea. "Let's swap places!" they cried.

The next night, before the dancers' last performance at the palace, the princess and the ballerina met up and changed clothes. "We leave tonight," said Ella. "We must meet later and swap back, or there will be terrible trouble."

Princess Rosalind put on Ella's costume and the jeweled mask. Ella put on the princess' pretty pink dress. The ballerina's mask meant that none of the other dancers noticed that the princess wasn't Ella. She tiptoed off to the palace and sure enough, nobody even glanced at her.

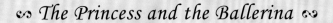

Rosalind had been practicing her dancing all day. When the curtain rose, she was very nervous. But she danced as she had never danced before. At the end of the performance, the audience clapped and cheered. Afterwards, Ella followed the king and queen quietly to the Banqueting Hall. She sat with them at a table, covered with all kinds of food. Luckily for Ella, the king and queen were so busy eating and talking, they didn't look at her too closely.

Ella had never seen such delicious food. She started eating before everyone else. She grabbed handfuls of grapes and ate a chicken drumstick with her hands, instead of using her gold knife and fork. When she drank milk, she got it all around her mouth. Then, without using a napkin, she wiped her mouth with her hand. The king and queen were shocked. "Rosalind, where are your manners?" the queen said. "Go straight to bed!"

Ella was marched upstairs to Rosalind's room. The queen was angry and locked the door, so Ella couldn't get out. Outside, the dancers' caravans were getting ready to move off. Ella could see them from her window. She had to reach them, or she would be left behind.

Ella opened the window of the bedroom and saw that she wasn't very high off the ground. She climbed out of the window and onto a ledge. The ledge was very thin, but Ella was used to balancing on her tiptoes. She looked for a way down into the gardens below.

Meanwhile, the dancers hadn't noticed that they were hiding a princess. "Ella, your dancing was a little sloppy tonight," said Ella's mother. "You will spend two hours practicing tonight before you have any supper. Then we leave the palace. Tomorrow, we perform at a castle far away."

Rosalind knew she had to escape back to her family, but she was surrounded by all the dancers and Ella's mother was watching. Luckily, they were inside the grounds of the castle and the princess knew all the secret passageways that led in and out of the palace. When no one was looking, she pressed a hidden button and a small door opened.

Rosalind slipped through the door and went down a secret passage that led into the palace garden. There, she saw Ella, balancing on the window ledge. Rosalind could almost reach out and grab her. "You'll have to jump, Ella," she said. "Don't worry, I'll catch you."

Ella dropped down from the ledge and Rosalind caught her. The two girls rolled onto the grass, laughing. Then they stood up and quickly swapped their clothes. "Being a princess is harder than it looks," said Ella. "Not as hard as being a dancer," laughed Rosalind.

By now, Ella's mother and the king and queen realized that their daughters were missing. They heard the girls' laughter and ran into the garden. "Ella, we're leaving," said her mother, "come on!" The princess and the ballerina smiled at each other and said goodbye.

The king and queen took Rosalind back into the palace. "I think we should spend more time together, Rosalind," said the queen. "Perhaps you could show us your dancing," added the king.

Ella's mother decided that her daughter spent far too much time dancing. "In future, Ella," she said, "you shall have more time to play."

After that, the princess and the ballerina were both much happier. Nobody ever found out that the ballerina had joined a royal banquet, or that the princess had danced on stage and they all lived happily ever after.

The Snow Queen

Once upon a time, there was a boy named Kay and a girl named Gerda. They were best friends and loved to play together among the flowers in Gerda's garden.

One winter's day, when they were playing outside in the snow, Kay tasted a snowflake that was falling from the sky. The snowflake was cursed by dark magic and suddenly, Kay felt his heart grow cold. Instead of seeing the goodness in all that was around him, he only noticed the things that were bad and ugly.

From that day on, Kay didn't play with Gerda. Instead, he preferred to look at snowflakes with his magnifying glass. "Snowflakes are much nicer than flowers," said Kay. "Flowers are boring!"

Poor Gerda was left alone, while Kay played on his sled with all the older boys. One day, a strange, white sleigh stopped nearby. It was pulled by two beautiful, white horses and Kay tied his sled to it. To his surprise, the sleigh sped off across the snow and pulled him along for many miles.

When it stopped, Kay saw a pale lady, dressed in white fur. "I am the Snow Queen," she said. "Come under my cloak to get warm." So Kay slipped under the cloak of the Snow Queen. As he did, his heart froze over. He forgot all about Gerda and the friends he had left behind.

The Snow Queen took Kay by the hand and they flew through the air. They landed in the frozen north, at the Snow Queen's ice palace, which had a great lake at the center. The palace was a mighty fortress of snow and ice and the Snow Queen made Kay a prisoner there. He had no memory of Gerda, or his old life.

"I must go on a long journey," said the Snow Queen. "By the time I get back, I want you to put all the ice on my lake back together." The ice on the Snow Queen's lake had split into hundreds of pieces, like a giant jigsaw puzzle. Kay sat by the frozen lake and moved the pieces around, but the puzzle was impossible to solve.

Meanwhile, Gerda spent her days looking everywhere for Kay. She spoke to the older boys, who told Gerda that Kay had gone north with a strange sleigh. So she walked and walked, through fields and forests. Wherever Gerda went, she asked about Kay, but nobody had seen him.

After many adventures, Gerda found herself in a cold land. There was nobody to be seen, except for a herd of reindeer. As they trotted past, she called out to them, "Have you seen my friend, Kay?"

The reindeer walked past, as if they hadn't heard her, except for one old reindeer. "I have seen this boy," he said. "He was being carried on a sleigh with the Snow Queen. She traps boys and keeps them in her ice palace."

When she heard this, Gerda wept. "I'll never find Kay," she said. "Don't worry," replied the reindeer. "The palace is far to the north. I can travel very fast through snow and ice, so I will take you there."

Gerda climbed onto the reindeer's warm and furry back, then they galloped far to the north. At first, there were thick forests on the hills around them but soon, the grass disappeared and the trees died away. After a while, they were surrounded by snow and ice.

Gerda and the reindeer traveled for countless days, until it was so cold that Gerda could barely move. Ahead of them, the night sky was filled with the shimmering, glowing rainbow bands of the northern lights, that lit the reindeer's way.

Finally, Gerda and the reindeer reached the North Pole. They found a great palace that looked as if it had been carved from a single block of ice. "This must be the ice palace," said Gerda.

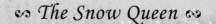

As Gerda approached, there was a strange, low, rumbling noise. The sound grew louder and then, suddenly, ice creatures, shaped like great bears, rose up from the snow and stood guard at the entrance to the palace. Gerda was afraid, but she found that her hot breath melted the creatures and she passed safely through the entrance to the palace.

Inside, the ice palace was vast and silent. Gerda marveled at the huge, freezing halls, whose ceilings seemed to stretch upwards to the sky. She shivered in the cold. "I must find Kay," whispered Gerda and she continued to search the Snow Queen's palace.

There were giant, empty halls everywhere. Gerda walked through them and found Kay sitting by the lake, moving pieces of ice around in a daze.

Gerda ran to Kay. She hugged him, but he didn't even notice her. He was too busy trying to solve the impossible puzzle the Snow Queen had set him. Gerda began to cry and her tears touched Kay's face. The warm tears melted all the ice around Kay's heart. He sat up and looked around, as if waking from a dream. "Oh Gerda!" he said, "I'm so glad you're here."

The two friends ran from the frozen palace. Its vast halls echoed with their footsteps. Outside, they climbed onto the reindeer's back and galloped off, before the Snow Queen could return.

It was a long and tiring journey. After many days, the weary friends arrived home, to find that it was summer and the flowers were in bloom. Kay and Gerda played together in the garden, just as they used to do and never again did the Snow Queen freeze Kay's heart.

Snow White

Long ago, there lived a king and queen who were overjoyed when they had a beautiful, baby girl. However, soon after the child was born, the queen died. The poor king was heartbroken. He held his baby daughter and looked at her. She had lips as red as blood, hair as black as night and skin as white as snow. "I shall name you Snow White," said the king.

A few years later, the king married again. Snow White's stepmother was beautiful, but also very cruel and vain. She was secretly a witch, who had great powers. The new queen owned a magic mirror, which answered any question that was asked of it.

Each day, Snow White's stepmother always asked the mirror the same question, "Mirror, mirror, on the wall, who is the fairest of them all?" The mirror always replied with the same answer, "You, my queen, are the fairest of them all."
This made the queen very happy. Secretly, she was jealous of Snow White and feared that the girl would grow to be more beautiful than herself.

One day, when Snow White had grown into a young woman, the queen asked the mirror her usual question, "Mirror, mirror, on the wall, who is the fairest of them all?"
This time, the mirror replied, "Snow White is the fairest of them all."

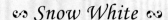
The queen flew into a jealous rage and decided to get rid of Snow White, once and for all. She summoned a huntsman. "Take Snow White into the forest and kill her!" she commanded. The huntsman didn't want to kill Snow White but, like everyone else in the castle, he was terrified of the wicked queen.

That night, the huntsman grabbed Snow White from her bed, while she was sleeping, and took her into the dark, dangerous forest. Even though the huntsman was cowardly, he wasn't evil and he couldn't kill Snow White. Instead, he put her down safely in the middle of the forest and warned her not to return to the castle.

Snow White wandered through the forest all night, getting more and more tired and frightened. As the first light of day broke through the twisted trees, she found a strange little cottage. She knocked, but nobody answered. Entering, she found seven little plates around a table, with seven little chairs, and seven little beds in the corner. Snow White was so tired, she lay on a bed and went to sleep.

When she awoke, Snow White saw seven dwarfs staring at her. At first, the dwarfs were angry that Snow White had come into their home. However, when Snow White explained her troubles, they said that she could stay. So Snow White lived in the little cottage with the seven dwarfs.

Meanwhile, the evil queen asked the mirror if she was the fairest of them all. "Snow White is the fairest of them all," replied the mirror. The jealous queen was furious and asked the mirror where Snow White was. The mirror told her about the little cottage, deep in the forest.

The queen used magic to disguise herself as an old woman. The next day, when the dwarfs were working, the queen went to the cottage with an armful of pretty clothes. "Try this pretty dress on, my dear," she cackled. Snow White tried the dress on, but the queen laced it up so tightly that Snow White could not breathe. She fell to the ground and lay still. The queen fled before the dwarfs could return. She was sure that Snow White was dead.

 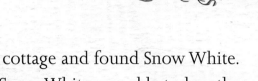

That evening, the dwarfs returned to the cottage and found Snow White. They quickly unlaced the deadly dress and Snow White was able to breathe again. The dwarfs were relieved that no harm had come to their friend.

That night, the queen questioned the magic mirror again, only to find out that Snow White was still alive. This time, her rage was terrible to see. She enchanted an apple, so that one side was full of deadly poison, but the other was safe to eat. The only thing that could break the spell was a kiss from Snow White's true love.

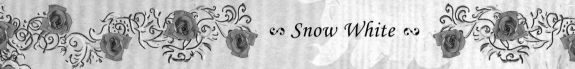
The next day, the queen returned to the cottage, in the magical disguise of a different old woman. "Have a bite of this tasty apple," she said. But this time, Snow White was suspicious and wouldn't touch it. "Look," said the queen, eating the side of the apple that was not poisoned. "See? It's tasty." Snow White took a bite from the poisoned side of the apple and fell down, as if she was dead.

This time, when the dwarfs returned, they couldn't wake Snow White. "She's dead!" they shouted. The dwarfs were very sad. They made Snow White a magnificent glass coffin and cried as they laid her in it.

Long years passed and the dwarfs guarded the coffin every day. Snow White stayed as beautiful as ever, as if she were only asleep.

One fine day, a handsome prince passed by the coffin. "Who is this beautiful girl?" he asked. "I must kiss her." He opened the coffin and kissed the girl's cheek. As he did, Snow White awoke. True love's kiss had broken the curse.

The prince took Snow White to his palace and they were married straight away. Snow White asked the seven dwarfs to join them and they all lived happily ever after.

Snow White

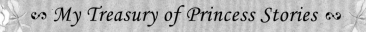

Sleeping Beauty

Once upon a time, a baby girl was born to a king and queen. She looked so bright and fair, they decided to name her 'Beauty' and a great celebration was held in her honor.

Because the queen was half-fairy, she invited three of her fairy cousins to give blessings to the baby. However, she forgot to invite one distant relative—a fairy with a very bad temper.

On the day of the blessings, the fairies gathered round the child's crib. "I give Beauty the gift of goodness and kindness," said the first fairy. "I give Beauty the gift of graceful dancing," said the second fairy.

However, before the third fairy could utter her blessing, a cold wind whirled around the crib. The angry fairy, who had not been invited, appeared. Her face was like thunder. "So, you're having a christening without me?" she snarled. "Now this child will have my present, whether you like it or not! I curse Beauty to prick her finger on her sixteenth birthday and die!" Suddenly, the wind whirled again and the fairy vanished.

Everyone was too shocked to speak. Finally, the third fairy spoke. "I have not given my gift yet," she said in a small voice. "It is not within my power to lift the curse laid on Beauty, but I can change it a little. My gift to you, Beauty, is this—you will not die on your sixteenth birthday, but you will sleep for a hundred years, until you are awakened by true love's first kiss."

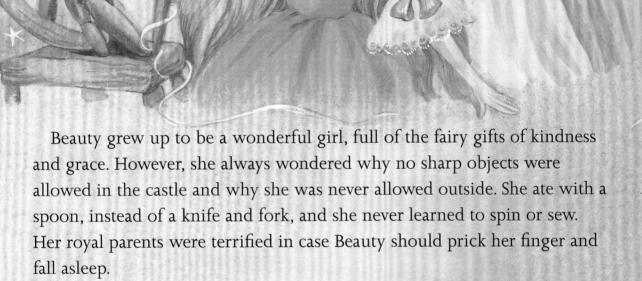

Beauty grew up to be a wonderful girl, full of the fairy gifts of kindness and grace. However, she always wondered why no sharp objects were allowed in the castle and why she was never allowed outside. She ate with a spoon, instead of a knife and fork, and she never learned to spin or sew. Her royal parents were terrified in case Beauty should prick her finger and fall asleep.

On the day of her sixteenth birthday, Beauty was exploring the castle. In one corner of the hall, she saw a little door that she had never noticed before. It led up a winding staircase, to a room in the highest tower of the castle. There, Beauty saw a woman sitting by a spinning wheel.

Beauty greeted the woman and asked what she was doing. "I'm spinning," replied the woman, who was the angry fairy in disguise. "Would you like to try spinning, my child?"

"Yes, please," said Beauty and she sat at the spinning wheel.
The fairy passed Beauty a sharp spindle, to wind the thread. Beauty took it
but, as she did, she pricked her finger. Instantly, Beauty slumped onto a dusty
old bed and fell into a deep, sleep.

As soon as Beauty began to sleep, a strange thing happened in the castle.
The king and queen, on their thrones, yawned and dozed off. The court
jester slumped to the floor and the cook fell asleep in the middle of
preparing dinner. Soon, everyone in the castle had drifted off to sleep.

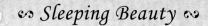

Around the castle moat, green vines began to sprout from the ground. In moments, the vines grew up and up and twined their way around the castle. Huge, sharp, thorns grew thickly. It was part of the third fairy's magic, to protect Beauty and the castle from harm.

When people in the outside world saw what had happened to the castle, they stayed away. Occasionally, an adventurer would come, seeking the riches of the sleeping king, but they were always turned back by the sharp thorns and the castle remained untouched.

One hundred years passed in silence, until a handsome prince rode by. He had stumbled upon the thorn-covered castle. "I must find out what is inside," said the prince. He drew his sword and cut straight through the thick tangle of thorns.

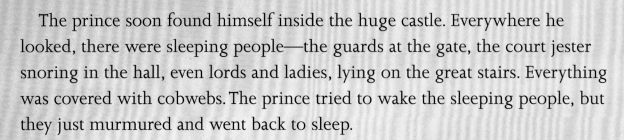

The prince soon found himself inside the huge castle. Everywhere he looked, there were sleeping people—the guards at the gate, the court jester snoring in the hall, even lords and ladies, lying on the great stairs. Everything was covered with cobwebs. The prince tried to wake the sleeping people, but they just murmured and went back to sleep.

As he passed through the Great Hall, the prince saw a little door standing open. It led to a tiny, winding staircase. Climbing the staircase, he found a room in the highest tower of the castle, with an old, cobwebbed spinning wheel, standing in one corner. On the dusty bed, lay the most beautiful girl he had ever seen. He leaned over and gave the girl a single kiss. Beauty stirred and opened her eyes. When she saw the prince, she fell instantly in love.

The spell was broken and the silent castle began to stir. The king and queen woke up, the jester started to juggle, and the cook began cooking. The whole castle had come back to life. The prince went to the king and asked him for his daughter's hand in marriage.

In no time at all, the people of the castle had recovered from their hundred years' sleep. The prince and Beauty were married and everyone lived happily ever after.

Twelve Dancing Princesses

A king once had twelve daughters. They were good daughters, except for one, very strange thing. Every night, the princesses left their shoes by their beds. Every morning, the shoes would be completely worn out. Whenever the king asked the princesses why this was, they giggled and ran off.

The king spent so much money on new shoes for his daughters, that the kingdom began to run out of money. The king decided that something had to be done. He issued a proclamation throughout the land, "Whoever can find out what happens to my daughters' shoes will become heir to the throne. He may also marry any of my daughters. But whoever fails to find out the secret in three days, will be banished."

One brave knight after another, vowed to find out the secret of the twelve dancing princesses. They tried to stay up all night, but when the sun came up, each one found that he had drifted into a deep sleep. The shoes were worn out and there was no clue as to how it had happened. These knights were banished, just as the king had promised.

One day, a soldier returned to the kingdom after a long time away. When he heard about the proclamation, he went to the king. "I will find out the princesses' secret," said the soldier. "I have spent my life fighting. A few princesses don't scare me."

While the soldier was walking back from the palace to his cottage, he met an old, wise woman and told her of his quest. "Here," said the wise woman, holding out her hands. "Take this cloak."

"What cloak?" asked the soldier.

"It is a cloak of invisibility," said the wise woman.

The soldier held the invisible cloak. Even though he couldn't see it, he could feel its soft material in his hands. "Pretend to be asleep when the princesses call you," said the wise woman. "Then, put on the cloak. However, make sure you don't eat or drink anything they give you."

The next night, after the princesses got ready for bed, the soldier stood guard over them. "Take this drink," said the eldest princess, handing the soldier a goblet. "It will warm you through the night." The soldier pretended to drink from the goblet, but he secretly poured it away and pretended to fall fast asleep.

The princesses sat up in bed and looked at the soldier. "Quick," said the eldest princess. "Let's go!" She opened a trap door in the floor and the princesses put on their shoes and went through it. Quickly slipping on the cloak of invisibility, the soldier followed them.

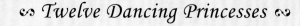

The princesses walked down a stairway into a dark tunnel. The soldier followed too closely and stepped on the youngest princess' dress. "Someone stepped on my dress!" she said, fearfully.
"Nonsense," said the eldest princess. "Hurry up, the princes are waiting."

The tunnel opened out into a wonderful land, filled with shining trees. As they passed through, the soldier saw that the leaves on the trees were made of silver. The soldier broke off a silver twig and the youngest princess heard the sound. "There is someone here," she said again, but the others told her not to be so silly.

Next, the princesses passed through a land where the trees had leaves made of gold. Then they visited a third land, where the trees had leaves of solid diamonds. The soldier had to shade his eyes, because the trees were so dazzling.

The princesses arrived at a wide, underground lake. There, twelve fairy princes, wearing glittering clothes, waited in twelve little boats. They rowed the princesses across the great lake. The soldier hid in the youngest princess' boat. No one noticed him because the magic cloak made him invisible.

When they reached the far shore, the soldier saw that they had traveled to Fairyland. Music started up from unseen instruments and the princes and the princesses danced all night. When they were tired, they drank from golden goblets.

At last, it was time to return. The soldier made sure he got back to the bedroom first. When the princesses arrived, the soldier pretended to be snoring. "It's a shame that this soldier must be banished when he fails to find out our secret," said the eldest, "but we have been bewitched and there is nothing we can do."

The next night, the soldier followed the princesses again. This time, he took a twig from one of the golden trees. On the third and last night, the soldier followed them and took a twig from a diamond tree. While the princesses danced, the soldier took a goblet and brought it back with him. The next day, the soldier came to the king. "Tell me the princesses' secret," the king said, "or I will banish you like the rest."

"The princesses have been bewitched by twelve fairy princes," said the soldier. When he showed the king and the princesses the twigs and the goblet, the spell on the princesses was broken. The king was no longer angry and hugged his daughters to him. "You may choose any of my daughters to marry," he said to the soldier.

The soldier thought for a long time. "The eldest is my choice," he said. "She is the cleverest of them all." The eldest princess married the soldier gladly and they lived happily ever after.

The Enchanted Orchard

A long time ago, a girl called Eleanor helped her father tend a garden in the grounds of a big castle. Even though the castle was owned by an unfriendly, bad tempered Duke, the garden was always full of flowers and people loved to walk and play.

The only part of the garden where Eleanor was not allowed to go was the old, walled orchard. It was full of tangled, overgrown apple trees. "It's a cursed place," Eleanor's father told her. "Don't go near the orchard. The duke has forbidden it."

As Eleanor was peering through the locked, orchard gates one day, she saw a girl dressed in white, walking among the trees. Eleanor was very surprised. Nobody was allowed in the orchard. She called to her father, but he was far away, at the other end of the garden. "I'll have to go in to get her," thought Eleanor, bravely. One corner of the high wall had fallen down a little and Eleanor scrambled over it. Her feet sounded very loud, as she crunched through the fallen leaves and small, rotten apples.

She saw the girl in white and ran to her, calling. But the trees around the girl seemed to shrink towards her, until the girl was trapped in a cage made of trees. Eleanor ran up to the cage. "I'll get you out," she said. "You cannot," said the girl, sadly. "I am the last princess of the castle. I was trapped here by my wicked uncle, the duke, many years ago. I cannot grow older, or escape."

Eleanor heard a deep, low voice, like the creaking of wood. Looking up, she saw that the trees themselves were looking at her. "We are cursed," they groaned. "We cannot let the princess go, until someone answers these two riddles in a single day."

"Here is the first riddle," said one tree. "What is soft, but brings forth hardness and inside the hardness is gold?"

A second tree spoke. "I have a door in your house and I eat your food, but you do not love me. What am I?"

"Don't worry, Princess," said Eleanor. "I'll find the answers to the riddles," And Eleanor ran as fast as she could out of the orchard.

Eleanor told her father and mother and they pondered the riddles all day. When Eleanor was feeding the family's chickens that night, she worked out the first riddle. "What's soft, but brings forth hardness and inside the hardness is gold? It's a hen! A hen's soft, but it lays an egg with a hard shell. Inside the egg is a golden yolk."

The second riddle was more difficult. Eleanor repeated it over and over again. "I have a door inside your house and eat your food, but you do not love me." The riddle was very puzzling. "Nothing has a door in our house," said Eleanor, looking around the little cottage. No matter how hard she tried, Eleanor couldn't think of the answer.

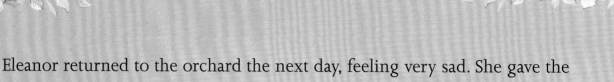

Eleanor returned to the orchard the next day, feeling very sad. She gave the first answer to the trees that held the princess. "The answer to the first riddle is a hen," she said.

"Correct," said the trees. Then Eleanor felt one of their branches grab her arm. "But what is the answer to the second riddle? Tell us, or we must imprison you forever with the princess."

Suddenly, a little mouse scurried over Eleanor's foot. "That's it," she whispered. "That's what has a door in our house—a mouse has a mousehole. It eats our food, but we do not love it. The second answer is a mouse," said Eleanor, loudly.

For a moment, there was no sound and then the trees parted to let the princess go. She hugged Eleanor in thanks. "At last, I am free. Here is a present for you." The princess gave Eleanor a silver necklace from around her neck.

When everyone learned what the duke had done, he was thrown out of the castle and the princess became its new owner. The orchard was no longer cursed and its trees grew the ripest, rosiest apples anyone had ever seen. Best of all, Eleanor and the princess became best friends and lived happily ever after.

East of the Sun, West of the Moon

Once upon a time, there was a man who lived in the north. He was so poor, he couldn't afford to feed his six daughters. One day, when he was sitting outside his cottage, wondering what to do, he saw a great, white bear approach. "Don't be afraid," the white bear said. "If you let your youngest daughter live with me, I will give you all the riches you desire."

The man went into the cottage and told his youngest daughter, Freya, who agreed to go with the bear. She climbed onto the bear's furry back and they galloped off, across the snow, to a golden palace, far away.

Freya was tired after the long journey and went straight to bed. Later on, she was surprised to see the bear come in and lay on another bed in the darkness. Freya even thought she saw him change his shape into a man, but she couldn't see his face.

Each night, the same thing happened. Freya went to bed and when the bear came in, he changed into a man. Freya thought it was very mysterious, but she was too afraid to question the bear, in case he got angry.

Some months later, Freya asked the bear if she could visit her family and take them some money. "You can," said the bear, "but remember one thing, you must promise not to talk to your mother about me."

The bear took Freya home, but she quickly forgot her promise. She told her mother about how the bear seemed to turn into a man. "He must be enchanted," said her mother. "Take this magic candle and see what he looks like."

When Freya returned to the palace, she lit the magic candle at night and saw the man's face. But three drops of magic wax dripped onto his shirt and he awoke. "You've broken your promise," he said. "I am a prince, cursed by a witch to be a white bear for a year and a day. I am in love with you, but now I must marry an ugly troll princess, who lives in a castle east of the sun, west of the moon."

Suddenly, the man and the castle disappeared. Freya was left on her own in the empty snow. She traveled for miles, until she saw an old woman with a golden apple. "Do you know how I can reach the castle that is east of the sun, west of the moon?" she asked.

"No," said the old woman. "But my sister might. Here, take this apple and borrow my best horse."

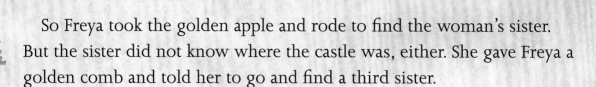

So Freya took the golden apple and rode to find the woman's sister. But the sister did not know where the castle was, either. She gave Freya a golden comb and told her to go and find a third sister.

So Freya rode on to a third old woman, who was holding a golden spindle. "The east wind might know the answer to your question," said the old woman, giving Freya the spindle, "ride to find him."

Freya found the east wind, but he didn't know where the castle was. He took Freya to his brothers, the south and west winds. They sent Freya to ask the cold north wind, which blew her all the way over the farthest ocean. There, she found the castle that was east of the sun, west of the moon.

At the castle, Freya saw the ugly troll princess. "I'll give you this golden apple, this golden comb, and this golden spindle if you'll let me see the prince," she said. The troll princess took them and let Freya in. Freya saw the prince and they embraced. "I have a plan," said the prince. "Take this potion and make sure you are inside the castle gates tomorrow."

The next day, Freya sneaked into the gates. She heard the prince say, "I will only marry the girl who can rub these three magic wax marks off my shirt." The troll princess scrubbed and scrubbed, but she couldn't rub them out. The princess ran up and rubbed them out easily with the potion. The troll princess was so angry that she ran far away from the castle.

Freya and the prince never saw the troll princess again. Soon, they were were married and lived happily ever after, in the castle that was east of the sun, west of the moon.

Beauty and the Beast

O nce, there was a poor merchant who had three lovely daughters. The youngest daughter was the kindest and most beautiful. Her name was Belle and she loved her father dearly.

One day, when the merchant had to go on a long journey, he asked his daughters what presents they would like him to bring back. The older sisters asked for dresses and jewels, but Belle knew that her father was poor and could not afford such finery. "I only want a rose, Father," she said.

The merchant journeyed far and wide. On the way back to his village, he was caught in a tremendous storm. Seeking shelter, he found a glittering palace. Nobody seemed to be in the palace, not even the humblest servant. Every one of the huge rooms was empty. The merchant sat down to rest and saw that a table was being magically laid for him. The plates and food flew through the air, as if they were being carried by invisible hands. The surprised merchant ate a hearty meal, then decided to continue on his way.

As he was leaving the palace, he saw a rose bush and remembered his promise to Belle. The merchant reached out and picked a single, red rose. Suddenly, there was a crash of thunder and a horrible beast appeared.

The beast had a bristly, hairy head like a wild boar's, with big teeth. Its hairy arms dragged on the ground, yet it wore clothes like a man. It snorted and snuffled. "How dare you steal from me!" cried the beast, in a rage. "Is this how you repay my hospitality?"

The merchant said he was very sorry and explained that he was only picking the rose for his daughter. But the beast wouldn't be calmed. "To pay for your crime, you must send this daughter to live with me. If you do not, I will come for you and take your life!"

The merchant hurried home and told his family what had happened. "I must go to the beast, or it will kill you," said Belle, sadly. The merchant wouldn't let Belle leave, but that night, she climbed out of her bedroom window and walked all the way to the palace, by herself.

The beast was waiting for her. At first, Belle was terrified by the sight of such an ugly monster, but the beast bowed and welcomed her politely. The invisible servants prepared them a delicious meal and they ate together. "This palace is your new home," grunted the beast. "There are many delights for you here. And now, I have a question to ask you. Will you marry me?"

Belle was shocked. "I can't marry you. I've only just met you," she said. The beast didn't look angry. He just nodded sadly and left.

That night, as Belle slept, she dreamed of a handsome prince. The prince seemed to be calling to her. "Save me! Please save me!" he cried.

The next day, Belle explored the palace. It was beautiful and magical. The invisible servants fetched her any food and drink she asked for. Every room was filled with beautiful dresses, gold and jewels, and all manner of fine objects. When she was bored, the invisible servants would carry her through the palace in an armchair. It was almost like flying!

Every evening, Belle and the beast would eat together and the beast would always ask Belle the same question. "Will you marry me?" But Belle always refused. Even though she couldn't dream of marrying such a hideous monster, she grew to love the beast. He gave her anything she asked for and in return, she was able to soften his rough manners and calm his dreadful temper.

Every night, Belle dreamt of the handsome prince. "How can I save you?" she would ask, but the prince would only say, "Don't trust appearances." There was something about the prince's eyes that reminded her of someone. But try as she might, she couldn't think who it was.

As the months passed, Belle began to miss her family. One night, she asked the beast if she could visit them for a while. "I cannot refuse you," said the beast. "But I love you so much, if you do not return soon, I shall die." The beast gave her a magic ring which transported her back home to her father and sisters.

Belle was so glad to see her family that she spent many days in their company. She almost forgot about the palace and the beast, until one night she had another dream. This time, it was the beast she saw, lying in the palace, almost dead from grief. "I have been so cruel!" cried Belle. She touched the magic ring and, in a flash, it transported her back to the palace in the blink of an eye.

Belle ran down the marble corridors and found the beast, just as he had been in her dream. He was lying on the floor, unmoving. She ran to him and cried, trying to wake him up. When her tears fell on his bristly face, he opened his eyes. "It is too late for me," he said. "I think I am going to die. Goodbye, Belle. It's a shame you didn't want to marry me."
"I will marry you, Beast!" cried Belle, hugging him tightly.

The moment she said the words, Belle felt the beast begin to change. He stumbled away and turned from her and when he turned back, he was no longer a beast. In his place was the handsome prince from her dreams.

The prince smiled at her. "I was cursed by a wicked witch to be a beast," he explained. "I have lived alone for many years, too afraid to go into the outside world because of my ugliness. The only way to break the curse was to find someone pure enough of heart to marry me, even though I was so horrible to look at."

Suddenly, all the servants became visible around him and they cheered the happy couple. The prince used the magic ring to bring Belle's father and her sisters to the castle. Soon after, the prince and Belle were married and they lived happily ever after.

The Frog Prince

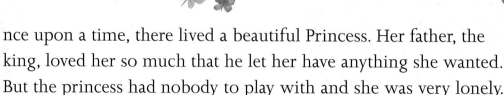

Once upon a time, there lived a beautiful Princess. Her father, the king, loved her so much that he let her have anything she wanted. But the princess had nobody to play with and she was very lonely. Sometimes, she would play on her own in the garden, with her favorite toy, a beautiful, golden ball.

One day, she was playing with the golden ball at the furthest end of the palace grounds. The princess threw the ball in the air to catch it, but missed. The ball splashed into the lake and sank without a trace. The heartbroken princess cried and cried.

"Excuse me, can I be of any help?" asked a deep, croaky voice. It was coming from the lake. A large, green frog popped his head out of the water and hopped onto the bank. "Why are you crying, Princess?" it asked.

The princess was so upset, she didn't think about how strange it was to meet a talking frog. Between sobs, she told the frog what had happened. "I'll get your ball back for you, Princess," said the frog. "But you have to promise me three things—you will let me eat from your plate, you will let me sleep in your bed, and you will give me a single kiss."

"How ridiculous!" thought the princess. "This frog could never bring my ball back, so what harm can there be in promising?" So the princess simply said, "Very well, I promise. A meal, a sleep, and a kiss."

Without another word, the frog dived back into the lake. A few moments later, it returned to the surface with the ball in its mouth. Overjoyed, the princess grabbed it and ran back into the palace. She didn't even stop to say "thank you" to the frog.

That evening, in the great Banqueting Hall, the princess sat down to dinner with her father, the king, surrounded by servants and courtiers. Suddenly, there was a soft knock on the great wooden door of the hall. One of the princess' servants opened the door and the frog from the lake hopped in.

"Hello, Princess," it croaked. "Remember your promise? You owe me a meal, a sleep, and a kiss."

The Princess was horrified. To think of that slimy creature in her beautiful, clean palace. She began to shoo the frog away, but the king stopped her. "If you made a promise," he said solemnly, "you have to keep it. Let the frog sit down next to you."

The princess was not happy at all, but she obeyed her father. The frog sat down next to her and ate from her special golden plate. The princess even had to put bits of food onto a golden fork so the frog could nibble at them. She could see the courtiers laughing when they thought she wasn't looking. "How awful," she thought. "This is so embarrassing."

When the meal was over, the frog asked the princess to take him to her bedroom. The princess gasped in horror and begged her father to make the frog go away. But the king shook his head. "You made a promise, my dear," he said. "And promises are even more important than kings."

So the princess went up to her bedroom in the tower. The frog hopped up the steps with her. All the people in the palace laughed when they saw them and the princess blushed angrily.

In her room, the frog jumped onto the bed and fell fast asleep. The princess lay down next to it, but she couldn't sleep a wink with the cold, damp frog lying next to her.

At long last, the sun came up and the frog awoke. "What a beautiful morning," it said, stretching its long back legs. "Please, princess, give me a kiss," said the frog, puckering its big green mouth.

The princess was revolted. She was ready to run away, but she remembered what her father, the king, had said, "If you made a promise, you have to keep it."

The princess reached over and gave the frog a kiss on its wide, green lips. Suddenly, the room seemed to turn upside down. The frog glowed and sparkled and in a flash of light, was gone and a handsome prince, dressed all in green, was standing there.

The prince bowed deeply. "Thank you, fair princess," he said. "Many years ago, a witch put a spell on me. I was turned into a frog and the only thing that would restore me was a kiss from a beautiful maiden. But I was so foul and ugly, nobody would even come near me. You kept your promise to me and now you have broken the spell."

The prince and princess rushed to find the king to tell him the good news.
The prince was asked to stay at the palace and soon, he asked for the
princess' hand in marriage. They were married and lived happily ever after
and the princess was never afraid to kiss the prince again.

The Princess and the Swan

Once upon a time, a beautiful princess married the handsome prince of a high mountain kingdom. However, after the wedding ceremony, the prince said to the princess, "I cannot stay with you at night. Every evening, I must leave our palace. However, every morning, I will return." The princess was surprised and upset. "Why do you do this?" she asked.

"Please do not ask," said the prince, "I can never tell you."

The prince made the princess promise that whatever happened, she must never follow him." The danger is too great," he said. At first, the princess said she would follow the prince anywhere, but the prince begged her to promise not to. Eventually, the princess relented. "I love you," she said, "and to love is to trust."

So that night, the prince left the palace and the princess wept into her pillow. The next morning, the prince returned, just as he had promised and they spent a wonderful day together. But the next night, the prince left again, and the princess was all alone until morning.

This continued for many months, until the princess could bear it no longer. One night, she secretly watched the prince walk off in the direction of an enormous lake, which lay in the hollow between two great mountains. "I cannot follow him, or I will break my promise," thought the princess. "But what if he is in danger and needs my help?"

The very next night, the princess found herself creeping down the palace stairs, after the prince, to see where he went. She followed him up hills and down valleys, through woods and fields, until he arrived at a black, marshy lake. There was an island in the middle of the lake, that gleamed silver in the moonlight. On the island was a tall man, in silver robes. Many beautiful white swans surrounded the island. The man raised his arms and the prince seemed to shrink and grow smaller and darker. In a moment, the prince was gone and in his place was a graceful, black swan.

The swan took to the water and the man on the island shouted, "Dance, swans! Follow the prince, your leader, as you must do every night!"

At his command, the swans began to cross the lake in slow, sweeping movements, with the black swan in the lead. The man on the island laughed and sat down to watch.

The swans danced in the water, until the sun began to rise across the mountains. The princess left quickly, so as not to be seen. She saw a single tear, drop from the black swan's eye.

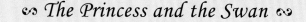

Back at home, the princess didn't know what to do, so she consulted a wise woman who lived near the palace. "The man on the island is a wicked enchanter," said the wise woman. "He has cursed your husband, who must dance for the enchanter every night. The only thing you can do to break the curse, is to destroy the wizard's heart. But it will be hard, because he keeps the heart in a diamond and the diamond is at the very bottom of the lake."

The princess was very frightened, but she knew what she had to do. The very next night, she waited until the prince had departed for the lake and she set out after him. Once the swans began their eerie dance, she knew she had to act. The princess dived into the water, to get the diamond, but the enchanter saw her and cast a magic spell that pulled her towards him.

"So, this is your wife," he said to the black swan. "Because she has broken her promise to you, your curse is doubled. You will be a swan forever!"

The princess cried in shame, but the black swan looked at her and said, "I forgive you. You loved me so much that you wanted to save me. Now, dive again, quickly."

The black swan turned to the enchanter and ran at him, pecking at him with its sharp beak and beating him with its wide wings. The enchanter cried out with rage. He turned from the swan and tried to grab the princess but, quick as a flash, she plunged into the lake and was soon out of his reach.

Holding her breath, the princess dived down and down, into the murky depths. Suddenly, she saw something glinting on the bottom of the lake.

The enchanter's heart was inside a gleaming diamond. Grabbing it, the princess swam back up, as fast as she could. She reached the surface and with all her might, the princess crushed the diamond in her hand.

There was a cracking noise and the diamond shattered. Instantly, the enchanter turned into a cloud of silver smoke that blew harmlessly away. The black swan shimmered and grew, until the prince was standing by the princess' side once more. She rushed into his arms and they held each other. When the princess let go of the prince, she saw that they were surrounded by men and women, all dressed in white.

"These were the other swans," explained the prince. "They are my loyal servants from my palace. The enchanter cursed them to stay here forever and he would have killed them all if I had not returned every night to dance with them. But now the curse is lifted and we are all free."

The Princess and the Swan

It was a joyous company that walked back to the castle that day.
Finally, the prince and his servants were free from the spell of the enchanter.
As for the enchanter, he was never seen again and the prince and princess
lived happily ever after.

The Fox Prince

Once upon a time, a princess named Arabella lived in a palace with her mother and father, the king and queen. The kingdom they ruled was very small and poor. Although the palace was made of marble and had many large rooms, the king and queen could not afford to keep many servants.

One day, a strange man came to the palace. He wore a wide hat with a yellow feather in it and a long, green cloak that reached down to his feet. He had a group of nine red-haired men with him. They also wore big cloaks and wide hats, so that nobody could see their faces clearly. They came into the palace and smiled at everyone. "I am Prince Reynard," said the man, bowing to the king and queen. "I bring you good news. Great riches will come to you."

The king was suspicious. "He doesn't look much like a prince to me," he whispered to the queen.
"Oh, but I assure you I am," said Prince Reynard, who must have had very good hearing. "I traveled to see you because I heard a legend about your palace. It is said that a great treasure is buried deep in the cellars of this castle. To reveal the treasure, everyone in the palace must gather in the cellar. Then, as if by magic, the treasure will appear."

The queen was very excited. "We are in great need of money," she said. "What harm can it do to try this?"
"It sounds very silly to me," said the king, "but if it brings us treasure, who am I to complain?"

So the king ordered everyone in the palace to gather in the Throne Room, ready to find the treasure.

As the king, the queen and the servants walked down to the cellar, Princess Arabella saw that Prince Reynard was hiding something beneath his cloak. It was big and bushy and had a white tip. "That looks just like a fox's tail," thought Princess Arabella! "Look, Mother," she said to the queen. "Prince Reynard has… "
"Not now, dear," interrupted the queen. "We're far too busy."

Arabella didn't want to go into the cellar. She ran and hid behind a curtain and watched as everyone else climbed down the steps. She noticed that Prince Reynard and his men stayed behind.

When the last person had gone into the cellar, Prince Reynard looked around quickly, gave a sly chuckle and promptly slammed the cellar door shut. He turned the key in the lock, so that the people of the palace could not get out. Prince Reynard jumped in the air and clicked his heels together. "Hooray!" he said. "My cunning plan has worked, my fox brothers, the palace is now ours."

Suddenly, Arabella realized that Prince Reynard wasn't a man at all. He was really a big, red fox, standing on its hind legs. His nine men threw off their cloaks and they were foxes, too. "Three cheers for the Fox Prince!" cried the other foxes and they carried the Fox Prince to the Throne Room.

Arabella tiptoed over to the cellar door, but the Fox Prince had taken the key. She spoke to the king through the keyhole. "Help!" called the king from inside the cellar. "There's no treasure! We're trapped! You must get the key, Arabella. Then we can chase the foxes away. But it won't be so easy to fool them, they are cunning beasts."

The foxes were all over the palace. They left muddy paw prints on the beds. They went into the kitchen and carried off the tastiest food. They opened the henhouses and chased the chickens. They frightened the horses in the stables and swung on the chandeliers.

Prince Reynard lounged on the throne, with the king's best crown on his head, while his fox servants brought him the daintiest dishes from the kitchens.

In the meantime, Arabella had thought of a plan. She walked into the throne room, where the foxes were dancing and drinking the palace's finest wine. "Hello, great Prince," said Arabella.

"Seize her!" cried the Fox Prince. "Put her in the cellar with the others."

"Wait," said Arabella. "I have a puzzle for you. But I don't think you're clever enough to solve it."

The Fox Prince was suddenly interested. He held up a paw to stop the other foxes grabbing the princess. He was a very proud fox and didn't like being told he wasn't clever. "I can solve any puzzle," he said. "Tell me what it is, princess."

Princess Arabella took a big, deep breath and told the foxes her puzzle. "In this palace are ten fine brushes that would clean up the mess you have made," she said. "But no matter where you look, they will always be behind you. If you can find them, I'll go into the cellar. If you can't, you have to let everyone out."

The foxes searched the palace, sniffing in every corner. But they couldn't find the brushes. "You're a liar," said the Fox Prince, after he returned to the throne room. He was panting from his search. "There are no such brushes." Arabella laughed. "The brushes are your own tails, you silly foxes!"
The Fox Prince felt behind him for his tail and laughed. "You win, princess," he admitted. He held out the cellar key for her.

Arabella took the key from the Fox Prince and ran to the cellar door. She unlocked it and the king and his servants quickly chased all the foxes out of the palace and into the woods. As the Fox Prince left, Arabella thought she heard him cry, "Goodbye, Arabella. It was a pleasure to be outfoxed by you!"

The Fox Prince never returned to the palace and the king, the queen, and Arabella, lived happily every after.

Thumbelina

Once upon a time, there was a little old woman who lived all alone. She longed for a child to keep her company. One day, she met an old witch hobbling down the road, outside her cottage. "Please, help me!" cried the old woman. "I want a little child so much!" The witch pushed a tiny barley seed into the old woman's hands. "Plant this and your wish will come true."

The old woman planted the seed and watered it carefully. Soon, it grew into a little green plant, with a single flower at its tip. The flower opened and inside sat a tiny, baby girl, no bigger than a thumb.

The old woman was overjoyed. "I shall call you Thumbelina," she said. She made Thumbelina a bed from half a walnut shell and put her in it. The tiny baby smiled and went straight to sleep.

As Thumbelina got older, she never got any taller, but she was the sweetest and kindest girl in the land. She loved to play in a bowl of water that the old woman put on the table. Thumbelina used a tulip petal as a boat and two stalks of grass for oars. She rowed around and around the bowl, as happy as could be.

One night, when Thumbelina was sleeping, a slimy toad crept through an open window and saw her. "What a pretty little girl," the toad said. "She will make a perfect wife for my son." The toad picked up Thumbelina and hopped out the window. He carried Thumbelina to the cold, muddy river bank and left her on a lily pad. "Soon, you will marry my son," he said and then hopped away.

Thumbelina was very frightened and began to cry. The fish in the river felt sorry for her and gnawed at the stem of the lily pad. Then a white butterfly let Thumbelina tie a thin reed around it. The butterfly pulled the lily pad into the middle of the river, where it floated downstream, far from the horrible, slimy toad.

Suddenly, something picked Thumbelina up. It was a big, black beetle, who carried Thumbelina to his home in the woods. "What a strange-looking creature you are," said the beetle. "Why, you only have two legs and no feelers at all. It must be horrible to be so ugly."

Thumbelina ran away from the insulting beetle and made herself a little home at the edge of the woods. She pulled a big leaf over her as a roof and made herself a bed from a couple of petals that she found. All summer, she lived in peace, sipping nectar from the flowers and making friends with the animals of the wood.

Then winter came and her little home was very cold. Snow started to fall. Thumbelina was so tiny, every snowflake that fell on her head felt like a big bucketful of snow.

Thumbelina was so cold, she was nearly freezing to death. She walked to a field where a field mouse lived. "Please let me come in to your burrow," she said, "or I'll freeze!"

The kind field mouse took her in and she spent the winter with him. Thumbelina liked the field mouse's burrow, but she didn't like the field mouse's friend, a boastful mole. "My burrow is much bigger than this," the mole said. "Thumbelina, you must come and live with me."

Thumbelina protested, but the mole wouldn't listen. He took her to his dark, clammy underground den. "Isn't it wonderful?" said the mole, but Thumbelina hated it.

One day, when Thumbelina was exploring the muddy tunnels, she found a swallow lying in the dark. He had become too cold and had fallen from the sky when he tried to fly south. Thumbelina nursed the swallow back to health, until spring arrived. "Thank you, Thumbelina," the swallow said. It fluttered out of the hole and into the sun.

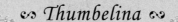

The mole wouldn't let Thumbelina go outside, in case she ran away. The summer months passed and soon autumn came. "It is time for us to marry," said the mole. "Then you can live with me forever."

No matter how much Thumbelina protested, the mole wouldn't listen. One day, when Thumbelina was sitting by the entrance to the burrow crying, she heard the flutter of wings. It was the swallow. "Come with me, quickly," the swallow chirped. "We swallows are flying south before the winter comes again."

Thumbelina jumped on the swallow's back and it flew off to join its brothers in the sky. The swallows' journey south was a long one and Thumbelina fell asleep on the swallow's soft back.

When she woke up, Thumbelina found that they were in a sunlit field, filled with poppies. She had never seen such lovely flowers before. Looking closer, Thumbelina saw a strange sight. Inside every flower, sat a tiny person. Some were men and some were women and they all had shimmering wings, like dragonflies. They were no bigger than Thumbelina.

The tiny man in the flower nearest Thumbelina was very handsome. He wore a shining crown. "I am the prince of the flower spirits," he said to Thumbelina. "You are the most beautiful girl I have ever met. Will you marry me?"

Thumbelina agreed immediately. All the flower spirits brought lovely gifts to their wedding. The best was a pair of shimmering wings for Thumbelina. She and the prince spent their days flying from flower to flower together and they lived happily every after.

The Twin Princesses

Once upon a time, there were twin princesses named Violet and Lily. Violet had short, dark hair. She loved to play games and explore the land outside their palace. Lily's hair was long and fair. She loved to stay inside, reading books and solving puzzles. Although the princesses were twins, they never agreed on anything.

One morning, an old beggar came to the palace. "Please, spare me some food," he said. But the princesses were too busy arguing to hear him. To the twins' amazement, the beggar threw off his disguise. He was really a mighty wizard. "If you had given me food, I would have rewarded you well," he said. "But you have made me angry! I curse this palace to sink into the ground when the sun goes down!"

The princesses said they were very sorry. They asked what they could do to lift the curse. "There are two crystals that are only found deep underground," said the wizard. "In the forest, by a spring, near an old oak tree, there is the entrance to a cave. The crystals lie in the sight of a statue, inside the cave. If you bring me these crystals by sunset, I will lift the curse. If not, the palace will be destroyed." Then the wizard vanished in a cloud of green smoke.

"Leave this to me," said Violet, "I'll find the crystals."

"You're no good at puzzles," said Lily. "I'll find them myself."

The Twin Princesses

Violet spent all morning exploring the forest. It was big and filled with springs and it took a long time for Violet to find the right one. Next to the spring, near an old oak tree, was the entrance to a cave.

Just as Violet was about to go into the cave, Lily joined her. "I found the spring and the oak tree on an old map in the palace library," she explained. "It was so much easier than searching the forest."

The princesses ran inside cave. The walls were covered with beautiful seams of gold and silver, but there were no crystals to be seen. Soon, the passage split into two paths. "I'm going left," said Lily.
"Then I'm going right," Violet said.

The two princesses wandered through the passages for what seemed like hours. They were cold and damp and it was difficult for them to see.

"I wish Violet were here," thought Lily, as she made her way through the passages.

"Lily would know how to get out," Violet thought to herself, as she tried to find her way to the statue.

Eventually, both princesses came out of the passages into an underground chamber, filled with silver and gold. They were very glad to see each other, although neither said so. At the back of the chamber was a big statue of a golden lion. The sisters searched all over, but they could not find any crystals.

The two sat at the base of the statue. "It's no good," said Violet, "there are no crystals here."

"Wait," said Lily, "it's a puzzle." The wizard said, "In *sight* of." She looked at the statue again and saw that its eyes were made of two round crystals. They were too high for Lily to reach, so Violet climbed up and got them.

"We've found the crystals," said Lily, "and we did it by working together."

The princesses dashed back through the cave to the spring. As they ran through the forest, they saw the sun was setting. When the princesses reached the palace, they saw that the ground around it had turned to mud. The palace was beginning to sink. They splashed through the mud and dashed into the palace courtyard. "Wait!" the princesses cried, holding up the crystals. "Wizard, where are you?"

The wizard appeared in a flash of light and they gave him the crystals. "Well done, Your Majesties," said the wizard. "Perhaps this will teach you to work together in the future." The wizard snapped his fingers and the mud around the palace turned back into solid earth. The palace rose up again, as if it had never moved.

The princesses were so happy that they had saved the palace. They agreed never to argue again. And they both lived happily ever after.

Rapunzel

Once upon a time, a poor couple lived next door to an enchantress. The enchantress had a garden full of fruit and vegetables. Every year, all the delicious carrots, lettuces, and apples lay on the ground and rotted. Meanwhile, the poor couple had hardly enough to eat.

One day, the poor man's wife was very hungry indeed. She was about to have a baby and needed to eat some food. Her husband climbed the wall and went into the enchantress' garden. He picked a big lettuce and took some juicy apples and carrots home to his wife. The man and his wife ate the food and it was delicious.

But the enchantress was very angry with the poor couple. "You have stolen from me," she said. "When your baby is born, I will take it from you." And sure enough, when a baby girl was born to the poor man and his wife, the wicked enchantress took her away.

The baby was named Rapunzel and she grew into a lovely young woman, with long, golden hair. She had a beautiful singing voice and even though the enchantress hated to hear her, Rapunzel sang all day long.

One day, the enchantress took Rapunzel to a tall tower in the middle of a forest. She cast a spell on the tower, so that anyone left alone in it could never escape. "This spell cannot be undone," cackled the enchantress. "You will live here forever and I will not have to listen to you sing!"

Sometimes, the enchantress came to visit Rapunzel. She would call out, "Rapunzel, Rapunzel, let down your hair." Rapunzel would unpin her long, golden hair and lower it out of the window, so the enchantress could climb up into the tower room. The enchantress gave Rapunzel a few scraps of food and made sure that nobody had managed to enter the tower. Then she would climb back down Rapunzel's hair and scurry home.

One morning, a prince was wandering through the forest and heard Rapunzel singing. He was entranced by her beautiful voice and followed it to the tower. He saw the enchantress call out, "Rapunzel, Rapunzel, let down your hair," and then climb up the golden locks.

When the enchantress had left, the prince called out, "Rapunzel, Rapunzel, let down your hair." Rapunzel, thinking the enchantress had returned, shook her hair out the window and the prince climbed up.

Rapunzel was very surprised to see a handsome prince, instead of the enchantress. Rapunzel and the prince fell in love and the prince vowed to rescue her. "I will visit you every night and bring you silk to weave into a ladder, so you can climb down the tower," the prince vowed.

Night after night, the prince brought more and more silk to the tower. It was such fine material that Rapunzel could hide it in her dress, so the enchantress did not see it when she came to visit. But the enchantress was clever. She saw that Rapunzel was happy and she did not know why. She asked Rapunzel many questions, but didn't get any answers.

The enchantress became angry and grabbed Rapunzel by her dress—and the silk came flying out in a long, billowing wave. "Wretch!" cried the enchantress. "You have tried my patience long enough!" The enchantress grabbed her scissors and cut off Rapunzel's long, golden hair. Then she muttered a spell and Rapunzel found herself far from the tower, in an unknown land, with no food or water, and no way to reach her prince.

Meanwhile, the enchantress waited in the tower for the prince to arrive. That night, he called out softly, "Rapunzel, Rapunzel, let down your hair." The enchantress lowered Rapunzel's hair. The prince climbed up to find the furious enchantress waiting for him. "So, you're the one who tried to steal my Rapunzel, are you?" she sneered.

The prince tried to grab the enchantress, but she pushed him backwards and he toppled out of the window, pulling Rapunzel's hair down with him. The prince landed in some bushes at the foot of the tower. He looked up at the enchantress who was shaking her fist and screaming with rage. She was alone in the tower and her spell could not be undone. The evil enchantress was trapped by her own magic.

The prince set off to look for Rapunzel. He wandered far and wide, searching towns and villages along the way. The prince often heard people talk of a girl with a beautiful voice, but no matter how hard he looked, he could never find her.

One day, after many disappointments, the prince had almost given up hope when he heard the sweet, familiar sound of Rapunzel singing. She had found work on a farm and was singing sadly as she carried water from the well. The prince ran to Rapunzel and they embraced.

The prince took Rapunzel home to see her parents. They were overjoyed at the return of their daughter. Soon after, the prince married Rapunzel and they lived happily ever after. As for the enchantress, she was trapped in the tower for the rest of her days and never troubled anyone, ever again.

The River Princess

O nce, there were three sisters, who lived all alone. Their names were First, Finest, and Fairest. First and Finest were proud and haughty. However, Fairest was as good as she was beautiful. The sisters were very poor, because their parents had both died and they hardly had any food to eat. Although Fairest was the youngest, she was also the cleverest and often found answers to problems that her two older sisters couldn't solve.

One day, First went to her two younger sisters,. "I am worried," she said. We have hardly any food and I fear that, if we do not get some soon, we will starve. I shall travel to see the River Princess, who lives in the wide river, to see if she can help us."

First set out for the river, whose banks were not far away. On her way, she saw a little beggar girl, begging for food. "Good mistress," said the beggar girl, "could you spare a crust?"
"I have no time," said First. And she bustled on her way.

When First reached the wide river, the water rose up and took the form of a beautiful maiden with a watery crown that glistened like sparkling diamonds. "River Princess," said First. "We are in need of food. Can you deliver some fish to our little cottage?"

The River Princess rose out of the water, like a living fountain. "Would you be so kind to those you meet on your travels? I think not. Be gone!" The River Princess knocked First into the river, so she had to return home, soaking wet. The beggar girl was really the River Princess in disguise.

Next, First's sister, Finest, decided to try her luck and set out towards the wide river. On her way, she saw a beggar girl who had fallen in a puddle of mud. "Please, help me up," called the beggar girl. But Finest was too vain. "What, get my clothes all muddy, just as I'm about to see the River Princess? Not likely," sniffed Finest and carried on her way.

When she reach the wide river, the River Princess rose up in a shower of sparkling, rainbow droplets. "We are in urgent need of food," said Finest. "Please, give us some of your fish—I'm sure you have more than you need."

The River Princess turned a dark, dangerous green, like the sea in a storm. "And would you lend a hand to help those you meet on your travels? I think not. Be gone!" The River Princess made a great wave of sludgy, slimy water rise up and cover Finest in thick mud. Finest ran home crying with anger.

"It's your turn, now," said First and Finest to Fairest, the next day. "I don't think the River Princess wants to be troubled by us," said Fairest, but she agreed to go all the same.

On her way to the wide river, Fairest met a beggar girl who had fallen over and was lying in a puddle of mud. "Help me, mistress!" cried the girl, reaching out with her arms.

Fairest was moved to pity by the poor beggar girl's plight. She pulled her out of the mud and gave the girl what little food she had. "You will be cold out here, all alone," said Fairest. "Here, take my cloak."

Fairest wrapped her cloak around the girl and went on her way. She looked back to see if the beggar girl was still there, but she had vanished.

When Fairest reached the river bank, she called out, "I humbly request an audience with the River Princess." The waters moved and the River Princess appeared. This time, her hair was the white of a foamy wave and all around her, river creatures glistened. "What do you want?" snapped the River Princess. "I have already told your sisters to go away!"

"Your Majesty," said Fairest, curtseying deeply, "is there any way I can help you in your watery realm? It is the least I can do to atone for my sisters' bad manners." The River Princess became clear and calm.

"Very well," she said, "my banks are becoming clogged with water weed. Can you remove it?"

Fairest spent all day wading by the river bank, pulling out handfuls of water weed. By the evening, she was muddy, drenched, and exhausted.

"A job well done," said the River Princess. "Do you have anything to ask of me?"

"No, Your Majesty," said Fairest, wiping the mud from her brow. "I ask for nothing."

The River Princess smiled. "Then return home, my child," she said, "and you will see the gift that I give to you."

Fairest walked home in the rain and arrived, as wet as First had been and as muddy as Finest had been. Her sisters laughed. "Now you know what it feels like," they snorted. But Fairest didn't say anything. Instead, she washed and went to bed.

Later on, in the dead of night, it so happened that a gang of thieves was passing. When they saw the sisters' cottage, they decided to break in and steal their last remaining possessions. As the robbers neared the cottage, they heard a crackling, swooshing sound. It was the sound of the river breaking its banks.

The water rose up in a great torrent and flowed all around the sisters' cottage. It rushed at the robbers and carried them far, far away, so they never troubled the sisters again.

When the sisters woke up in the morning, they found that the flood had subsided. It had reached right to their very door, but had come no further. Best of all, it had left a small stream running right past their house—and the stream was full of fish.

From that day onward, the sisters set nets in the stream and pulled out more than enough fish to eat. First and Finest mended their ways and thanked their sister for her hard work and kindness and the three sisters lived happily every after.

The Little Mermaid

Once upon a time, a little mermaid lived under the sea with her five sisters. Their father was the sea king and they lived in a wonderful palace made of shells and coral. The little mermaid was the best singer under the sea. When she sang, everyone in the sea palace stopped to listen to her beautiful voice.

However, despite all this, the little mermaid had a secret wish. She wanted to meet the people who lived on the land. Day after day, the little mermaid sat on a lonely rock, in the middle of the ocean and watched the ships pass by. She imagined what it must be like to live on dry land and walk on legs, instead of swimming with a fish's tail. Most of all, she longed to dance.

One day, the little mermaid saw a handsome prince and his servants on a passing ship. She was about to swim over to it, when a terrible storm rose up over the sea. Giant waves crashed over the decks and drove the ship onto the rocks, where it was wrecked.

The little mermaid saw that the prince was about to drown. She carried him safely to the shore, singing to him all the while. When some fishermen saw the prince on the shore and came to help him, the little mermaid splashed back into the sea in fright.

 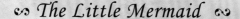
From that day on, the little mermaid thought only of the prince. She spent all her time wishing she could become human. In despair, she asked her sisters what to do. "Go to the sea-witch, who lives in the seaweed forest," they said. "She is clever and dangerous, but she may be able to help you."

So the little mermaid made the long journey to the sea-witch. Finally, she reached the seaweed forest. In the middle of the forest, in a hut made of bones, sat the sea-witch.

The little mermaid told the sea-witch her story. "I can make you human," said the sly old woman. "In return, I will take your most valuable possession—your voice." The sea-witch gave the mermaid a potion. "Go to the land and drink this," she said. "It will take your voice away, but give you legs, instead of a fish's tail. If the prince does not marry you, you will turn back into a mermaid and never be human again."

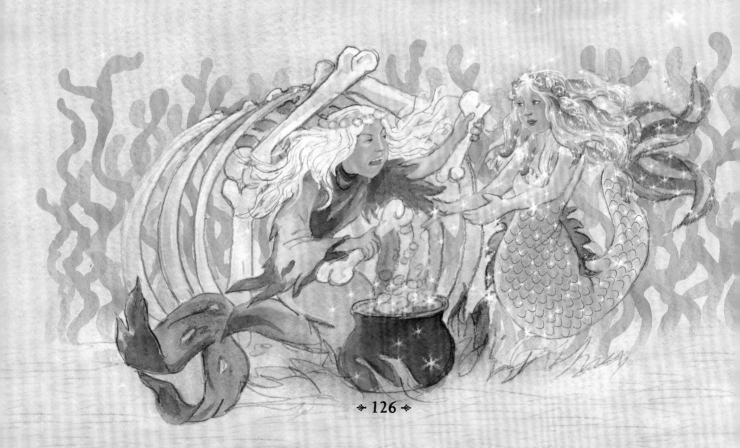

The little mermaid swam straight to the prince's palace. On the beach, nearby, she took the potion and found she could no longer speak or sing. Looking down, she found she had two legs instead of a tail. The little mermaid was so shocked that she fainted and when she awoke, the prince was standing over her.

The prince was very kind to the little mermaid. He took her to live at the palace and gave her food and fine clothes. The little mermaid found that she could dance on her new legs. She followed the prince everywhere and they spent all their time together.

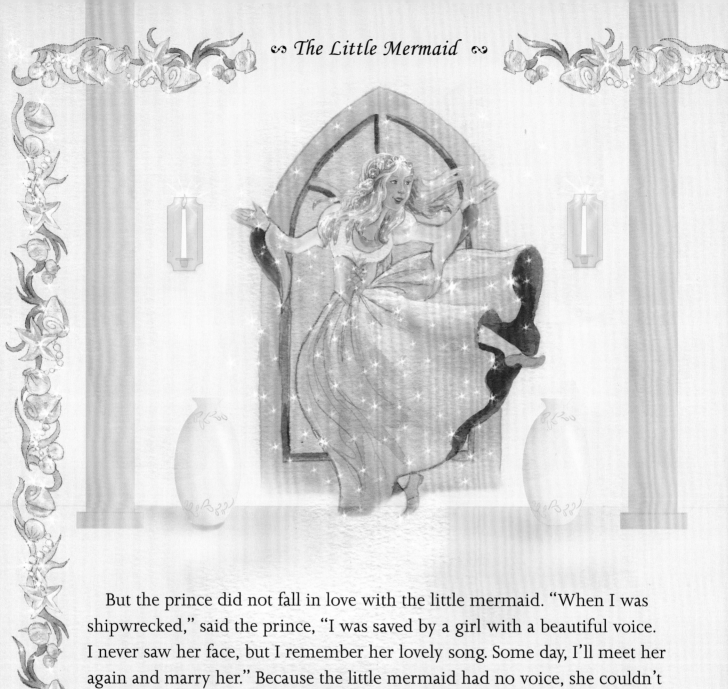

But the prince did not fall in love with the little mermaid. "When I was shipwrecked," said the prince, "I was saved by a girl with a beautiful voice. I never saw her face, but I remember her lovely song. Some day, I'll meet her again and marry her." Because the little mermaid had no voice, she couldn't tell the prince that she was the one who had saved him.

The prince's father, the king, ordered him to sail to a foreign country to marry a princess who lived there. When the little mermaid found out, her heart ached. "If only there were a way to show the prince that it's me he should marry," she thought, desperately. "If he kisses the princess, I will become a mermaid and I'll never see him again."

The little mermaid traveled with the prince on his ship. It sailed to the foreign land, where the prince met the princess his father had chosen for him. She was beautiful, but she was also very cold and stern. One day, the little mermaid saw the prince and the princess talking. The princess kissed the prince on the lips and the little mermaid's heart broke.

The little mermaid dived back into the sea. As the water closed over her head, she felt her legs become a fish's tail again. She swam back to her father's palace, where her sisters and her father were waiting. The little mermaid found that she had regained her voice, so she told them everything that had happened. Then she went to sit and sing sadly on her lonely rock.

One day, the prince's ship went past the rock. The prince heard the sound of singing. Looking out, he saw the little mermaid. "You saved me!" he cried. He jumped from the ship and swam to the rock. "I never married the princess," he said. "As soon as you were gone, I knew that it was you I loved. I don't care that you're a mermaid."

The prince took the little mermaid ashore. When he kissed her, the little mermaid found that she had legs again. Soon after, she married the prince and became human forever. The little mermaid's family often came to visit her and she lived with her prince, happily ever after.

The Flower Princess

Once upon a time, a beautiful princess lived in a palace with a magnificent garden. In the summer, the garden burst into life. In the winter, it sparkled with snow and ice. Springtime brought blooms and blossoms of every kind and all who saw them were amazed. At the heart of the garden, stood the tallest tree in the land.

More than anything else, the princess loved to spend time digging and planting flowers. Many rich princes came to try and win her hand in marriage, but she ignored them and tended her plants instead.

Every day, a young gardener helped the princess. He was in love with her, but she was so dazzled by the beauty of the flowers in the garden, she hardly noticed him.

Eventually, the king and queen decided it was time for their daughter to marry and invited two rich princes to visit. One prince was very fat and nervous-looking and the other prince was thin and delicate. They went to speak to the princess, who was outside, near the tallest tree.

"If I must marry, I must," said the princess, wiping her hands on her apron. "But I have one request. I will marry the man who can climb this tree and bring me the single blossom that grows at its highest point."

The two princes looked up at the tree. It was so high that they could hardly see the top of it. The blossom was just a flash of pink in the sky. There weren't many low branches on the tree, either. It was going to be very difficult to climb. But the princes both wanted to marry the princess, because they knew that, whoever married her, would one day be king.

The fat prince was the first to speak. "I will climb the tree and fetch the blossom," he declared, then he clambered awkwardly up into the lower branches.

By the time he got halfway up the tree, the fat prince was red-faced and out of breath. Trying not to fall, he scrambled up to the very top and found the pink blossom. Beside the blossom, sat a big, golden eagle. The eagle had great, curved claws and a sharp, dangerous-looking beak. The prince was so frightened, he scampered back down the tree as fast as he could. Then he quickly said goodbye and left the palace forever.

The next day, the thin prince tried to climb the tree. He was much stronger and fitter than the fat prince and was glad that the princess was there to see him. He slung ropes on to the branches and climbed them speedily, until he was almost at the top. The eagle stared down at him with its hard, gold eyes.

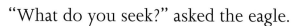

"What do you seek?" asked the eagle.

"I seek the blossom," replied the thin prince.

"Why do you seek it?" the eagle asked.

"So that I can become king one day," said the thin prince.

"That was the wrong answer," cawed the eagle. It launched itself at the thin prince and chased him all the way down the tree, out of the garden, and away from the palace for good.

The princess began to cry. She was very sad that neither of the princes had brought her the blossom. "It is so beautiful," she said, sadly. "I would have loved to smell its perfume and feel its delicate petals."

The young gardener overheard the princess and decided to get the blossom for her. He put his tools down and began to climb the tree. Without any ropes to help him, it was a hard climb.

When he reached the top of the tree, the eagle spread its wings and stared at him sternly. "What do you seek?" it asked.
"The blossom, please," replied the gardener.
"Why do you seek it?" asked the eagle.

The gardener thought for a moment and then he spoke. "I am just a simple gardener," he said. "However, I love the princess more than anyone in the world. Her heart was set on having this blossom and neither of the princes were able to get it for her. Now she is sad and all I want to do is to make her happy."

"That is the right answer," said the eagle. "Now climb onto my back and take the blossom."

The gardener climbed on the eagle's back and picked the pink blossom. As soon as he did, the eagle began to magically grow in size, until it was gigantic. Suddenly, the eagle spread its great wings and glided down, to the bottom of the tree, where the princess stood.

The princess couldn't believe her eyes. She was amazed to see the gardener, flying on the giant eagle's back, holding the blossom. She blushed as he knelt and gave it to her. It was then that the princess realized something. "I have loved you all along, my kind and brave gardener," she said.

The princess and the gardener were married soon after. Every day, they continued to work in the garden together. When they became king and queen, they covered the whole kingdom with beautiful flowers.

The Princess and the Pea

O nce, there lived a prince who wanted to marry. He traveled all around the world and met many princesses, but he didn't fall in love with any of them. Some were too proud and arrogant, while others were rude or thoughtless. "Finding a wife is so hard," the prince sighed. "If only I could meet a princess who was kind and sensitive."

After his travels, the prince returned to his hometown, where his parents, the king and queen, greeted him. "Don't worry," the queen said, "I'm sure you'll meet the right princess, one day."

That night, there was a terrible storm. Thunder crashed and lightning flashed. Inside the palace, the king and queen were just about to go to bed when there was a knock at the door. The king opened it to find a pretty young woman standing on the doorstep. She was soaked to the skin.

The queen sat the young woman in front of the fire to dry her clothes. "But why have you come here, my dear?" she asked.
"I am a poor servant girl, looking for work," replied the young woman. "Please don't turn me away."

The prince had heard the knocking and came to see who it was. When he saw the girl, he fell instantly in love with her. The prince sat and talked with the young woman for a long time. "I wish she were a princess," he thought. "I would marry her straight away."

The Princess and the Pea

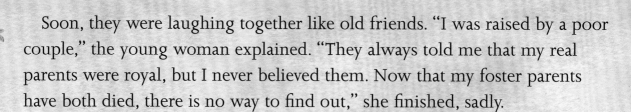

Soon, they were laughing together like old friends. "I was raised by a poor couple," the young woman explained. "They always told me that my real parents were royal, but I never believed them. Now that my foster parents have both died, there is no way to find out," she finished, sadly.

That night, the queen had a bed prepared with twenty mattresses, piled high, on top of each other. "This girl looks like a princess and she acts like a princess," thought the queen. "She must have royal blood and I think I know how to find out." She placed a single pea under the bottom mattress and sent a servant to fetch the young woman.

The queen showed the young woman into the bedroom and put a ladder against the side of the mattresses. "You can sleep here tonight," she said. The young woman thought it was a very strange way to spend the night. However, she was too polite to complain and climbed up the ladder.

The princess lay down on the mattresses and tried to go to sleep, but it was no good. No matter how she tossed and turned, she could feel something under the mattresses. It kept her awake the whole night. When the sun shone through the windows in the morning, she still felt tired. She climbed down the ladder and went out into the hall. "Did you have a good night's sleep?" asked the queen.

"No," said the young woman, shyly. "I think there was something under the mattresses, it felt like a hard lump. I was tossing and turning all night." At these words, the queen nodded and smiled to herself.

That afternoon, the queen went for a walk with the prince. "I am in love with the servant girl, mother," he said. "I just wish that she was a princess, instead of a servant girl." The prince looked very sad.

The queen smiled at her son. "Don't worry," she said. "The girl really is a true princess. Only someone with royal blood could be delicate enough to feel a single pea under twenty mattresses."

The prince was overjoyed at this happy news. He rushed back into the palace to find the princess. As soon as he saw her, he got down on one knee and asked for her hand in marriage. She accepted gladly, for she had fallen in love with the prince when she first set eyes on him.

The prince and the princess were married in the castle and everyone had a great celebration. The princess never did find out why she had to sleep on twenty mattresses, but she and the prince lived happily ever after anyway.

Cinderella

Once upon a time, there was a man who had a beautiful wife and a lovely daughter, called Ella. When his wife died, the man married another woman, who had two daughters of her own. They became Ella's stepsisters, but they were jealous of her and treated her like a servant. Poor Ella had to wear old, tattered clothes and do all the housework.

One day, Ella was in the kitchen, cleaning out the grate, when the two stepsisters came to see her. Ella's ragged clothes were stained and her face was covered in soot. "Look how dirty she is," cried one sister, fluttering her fan. "She's covered with ashes and cinders."

"We should call her Cinder-Ella!" said the other sister.

From that moment on, Ella became known as Cinderella.

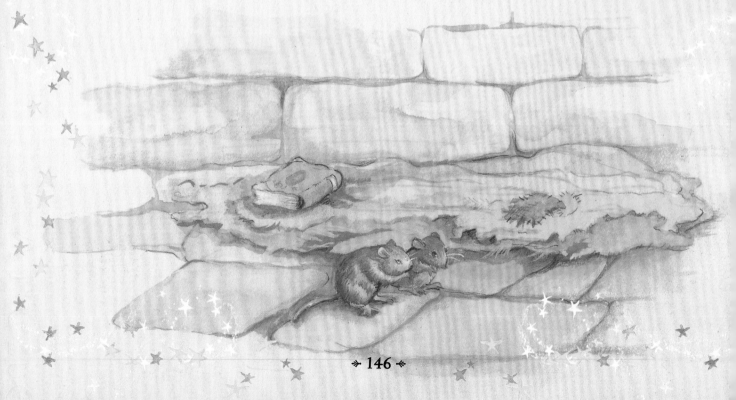

One day, news arrived at the house that the prince of the land was going to hold a Grand Ball at the palace. Cinderella's father made sure that his new wife, as well as Cinderella and her two stepsisters, were invited. But when the invitations came, the sisters tore up Cinderella's before she saw it. "Too bad," they said, "the prince doesn't want you in his beautiful palace."

When the night of the ball came, Cinderella had to help her stepmother and her stepsisters dress in their fancy gowns. Then she was sent back to the kitchen, to do all the washing, while they left for the ball. When all the work was done, Cinderella sat in the cold kitchen and cried. "I'm so sad and lonely," she said. "Won't anyone help me?"

The chimney of the big kitchen fireplace began to glow and sparkle, then something bright rushed out. A sparking, fizzing light circled the kitchen and a kind-looking fairy appeared, in a shower of sparks.
"Who are you?" asked Cinderella, in surprise.
"I'm your Fairy Godmother," answered the fairy, "and you look in need of help. What can I do for you?"

Cinderella explained that she wasn't allowed to go to the Grand Ball.
"Don't worry," said the Fairy Godmother, "you shall go to the ball!"
"But how can I go dressed in these rags?" asked Cinderella.
"A little magic will fix that," said the fairy godmother, sweetly." She waved her wand around Cinderella's head and her rags fluttered and flapped and swished and swelled, until they had turned into the most amazing ballgown Cinderella had ever seen. It even had a pair of glass slippers to match.

"Of course, you'll need to get to the ball," added the Fairy Godmother. She waved her wand over a pumpkin and it became a magnificent, sparkly, gold coach. Cinderella was amazed and thrilled to see the wonderful coach.

Next, the Fairy Godmother searched around the garden and found a lizard and four mice. She waved her wand over them and they were transformed into a coachman and four beautiful horses. "Now you can go to the ball," said the Fairy Godmother. "But remember, all my magic stops at midnight. So make sure that you are back here before then."

When Cinderella entered the ball at the palace, all eyes were upon her. The handsome prince took one look at her and fell instantly in love. He spent every minute of the night dancing with her.

Cinderella enjoyed herself so much, she forgot to watch the big clock that hung at one end of the ballroom. "I am falling in love with you," the prince told Cinderella, as they danced. "Do you love me because of my fine clothes?" asked Cinderella.

"I would love you, even if you were in rags," said the prince.

Suddenly, the clock began to strike midnight. Terrified of showing herself in her dirty rags, Cinderella broke free of the prince and ran out of the palace. In her haste, she left behind one of her glass slippers. As she was running down the palace steps, the gown turned back into rags, the coach became a pumpkin again, and the rats and lizard scuttled away. Cinderella ran back to her house and nobody knew that she had ever left it.

The prince swore that he would find the owner of the slipper. "The girl whose foot fits this slipper is the girl I shall marry," he said. The prince and his pages visited every house in the land and every girl, in every house, tried on the slipper. But it was so small and dainty, nobody's foot would fit into it.

At last, the prince came to Cinderella's house. "He mustn't see you," her stepmother said, so the sisters locked Cinderella in the coal cellar and was hidden from the prince. The two sisters both tried to make the shoe fit but, no matter how hard they squeezed, they couldn't squash their big feet into the tiny, delicate, glass slipper.

The prince was ready to leave when he heard knocking coming from the cellar door. Opening it, he was surprised to see a young girl dressed in rags and covered in ash and coal dust. "Let this girl try on the slipper," said the prince.

Cinderella tried the slipper on and her little foot slipped into it perfectly. The prince knew immediately that Cinderella was the girl he had danced with at the palace.

"Will you marry me and be my queen?" asked the prince. Cinderella had never felt so happy and accepted joyfully. The prince banished the wicked stepmother and the stepsisters to a faraway land and Cinderella and the prince were married without delay. Cinderella's father came to live with them in the Prince's palace and all three of them lived happily ever after.

The Princess' Song

A long time ago, in a faraway land, there lived a good and wise queen who loved to sing. Her kingdom was conquered by an evil king and the queen was cast out of her castle. The queen had a baby daughter, called Melody. She knew that Melody would be in danger if the evil king found her, so the queen gave the baby to a poor farmer and his wife. "Keep her safe from the king," said the queen.

A passing fortune-teller saw the queen saying goodbye to her baby. "One day, this child will rule the land," said the fortune-teller. The queen felt very sad, she said goodbye to her baby and sang a song, "Worry not, in days to come. The princess will return to claim her own."

The farmer and his wife already had two little boys, but they took care of the queen's child and brought her up as their own. Years passed and Melody grew to be a kind and beautiful girl.

Melody's stepbrothers grew to be strong boys, but they were jealous of her because she was a princess. The brothers called her names and made her clean the pigsty and work in the fields. However, Melody always stayed cheerful and would often sing to herself. She had a voice even purer and more lovely than her mother, the queen.

In time, the evil king died and his son ruled the kingdom. The new king was much kinder and nobler than his father. He loved singing and dancing. Wandering minstrels and acrobats were always welcome at the castle.

One day, the king decided to hold a contest to find the best singers and dancers in the land. His messengers went to tell the people of the kingdom. "The winners will each get a medal of solid gold!" they shouted.

The farmer and his wife thought that Melody had the most beautiful voice they had ever heard. They insisted that she enter the contest, so Melody began to practice her singing.

The brothers were even more jealous of Melody, now. They wanted to stop her winning the contest, so they went to a wicked wizard and bought a potion of forgetfulness. Whoever drank it would forget everything they had just learned. "Be sure to drink this before you sing," said the brothers to Melody. "It is a special potion that will improve your voice."

Melody spent day after day learning to sing the sweetest and loveliest songs. She sang while she dug in the fields and while she tended the sheep on the farm.

At last, the day of the contest came. There were singers, dancers, acrobats, and storytellers. There was even a circus with fire-eaters, jugglers, and horse riders. They had all come to win the prizes.

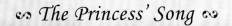

The young king sat on his throne, looking bored. One by one, the minstrels and puppeteers stood in front of him and performed. The king didn't even smile when he saw them. "This is extremely dull," he said. "I have seen all these people before. I wish there were one who was different!"

Finally, it was Melody's turn to perform in front of the king. She uncorked the potion that the brothers had given her and drank it in one go. Then she stepped out in front of the throne. She was so nervous that her hands were shaking.

"Sing," said the king, hardly bothering to look at her.

Melody took a deep breath and found that she had forgotten every single one of the songs she had learned. She stood there, fearful and wide-eyed. Then she remembered one song. It was the one the queen had sung to her when she was a baby. She sang, "Worry not, in days to come. The princess will return to claim her own."

Everyone in the castle stopped to listen. They had never heard such a beautiful sound. When the king heard the words of Melody's song, he knew that she must be the lost princess. He jumped from his throne and knelt on one knee in front of her. "Marry me," he said, "and we can rule the kingdom together."

Melody married the king and there was great rejoicing throughout the kingdom. They lived happily ever after till the end of their days and the castle was always filled with joyful song.